Friends
Are Like
That

Friends Are Like That

by Elizabeth Van Steenwyk

illustrated by Ray Keane

Published by Willowisp Press
801 94th Avenue North, St. Petersburg, Florida 33702

Copyright © 1988 by Willowisp Press,
a division of PAGES, Inc.

Printed in the United States of America

4 6 8 10 9 7 5 3

ISBN 0-87406-290-X

980218

One

KRISTI Cameron opened the door of the South Bay Skating Club and stepped inside. The cold air from the ice rink hit her cheeks and made her energy soar. She knew that when she skated out on the rink and heard the scrape of blades on ice, her feelings would leap right through the ceiling.

Every day, Kristi enjoyed going to practice at the rink. Some kids complained about the hard work, but not Kristi. She loved everything about figure skating.

"Hi, Kristi." Becky Marshall waved to her from the rink. "Congratulations. I heard you passed your fourth test. I knew you'd be the first one in our bunch to move up and skate at the novice level."

"Thanks, Becky." Kristi threw her skate bag on a bench. Then she dug out her white figure skates and began to put them on.

Becky did a spiral to the edge of the rink. Then she leaned against the railing that surrounded it. "How does it feel to be the number one novice at South Bay?"

Becky was teasing her, Kristi knew, but it was a nice tease. It felt great to be skating at the novice level. Maybe someday soon she would even be the best novice skater in the whole region. If she practiced really hard between now and the competition, she might be able to do it. She might be able to win! Then maybe she'd get her picture in the newspaper, like an Olympic figure-skating star. "YOUNG LOCAL SKATER, KRISTI CAMERON, FIRST IN NOVICE COMPETITION," the headlines would say. That's it, she thought. That's what I want more than anything—to be first in novice in the whole region.

She wondered if that would make her mother pay attention to her again. Probably not, Kristi thought. All summer, since the divorce, her mom had been involved in other things.

"Hurry up, number one," Becky called. "I need some help. If my coach sees what I just did on the ice, he'd kill me." She whirled off across the rink.

"I'll be there in a second," Kristi called back. She laced her skates tightly over her ankles. Then she slipped skateguards on her skates to protect them.

Kristi collected all her belongings and jammed them into her skate bag. Then she headed for her locker.

"Hey, Kristi, heard the news?"

She jumped and turned around. "Matt, you ought to put bells on your skates so I'll hear you coming."

"It's more fun to watch you jump." Matt's green eyes shot off sparks of mischief. "Know what?" he asked. "Pretty soon, I'll have another

novice skater around here to scare."

"What are you talking about?" Other kids skated at the novice level at South Bay. Kristi knew she wasn't the only one. She stopped by her locker and began to unlock it.

"I mean a *real* novice skater. Someone to give you some competition."

Kristi turned around. She felt her face crinkle up. "Matt Stevens, if you don't tell me what you're talking about, I'll trip you on the ice, first chance I get."

He laughed, then his face grew serious. "No kidding, I thought you'd have heard by now. Sara Mars is starting today."

"Sara Mars?" Kristi forgot her combination numbers and had to start over.

"Yeah," Matt said. He leaned against the next locker. "I was in the manager's office yesterday afternoon when the phone rang. I could hear this woman's voice talking and talking, and Mr. Billings never had a chance to say anything. He couldn't stop her long enough to tell me to leave.

So naturally, I stayed," he finished.

Matt grinned, waiting for Kristi to say something. She tried to find the words that would sound right. But there weren't any. How could she tell Matt or anyone else about how nervous she was feeling right now? Sara Mars would be skating at this club! She was the best novice skater in the midwest. Everyone involved with skating said she might even make the Olympics someday.

"Hey, what's the matter?" Matt gave her a poke. "You're not worried about competing against Sara, are you?"

"Competing? Do you even think that I'll be competition for her? No way! Sara Mars is the midwest novice champion. Even if she did hurt her leg last year, she's still got to be the best novice skater around. Besides, I read in *Skate and Spin* that her leg's okay now. She'll skate right by me in the regionals so fast I won't even see her!"

Matt grinned again and cocked his head to the

side. "Maybe. That is if Sara really is back in shape." He headed for the rink. "I have to run. See you at lunch."

Kristi put her bag inside the locker and closed the door. The great feeling she'd had when she entered the rink had disappeared. Imagine Sara Mars and me on the same rink, she thought. She stopped to look at her reflection in the soft-drink machine and pulled back a few stubborn curls that had slipped out from under her headband. Suddenly the full meaning of Matt's words hit her.

Imagine Sara Mars and me in the same competition! Just when I had a chance to win the regional novice competition, the midwestern champion moves to my region. We'll be skating for the same title. I won't stand a chance.

Kristi tried to smile at the blue-eyed, sandy-haired girl reflected in the shine of the soft-drink machine. But the girl refused to smile back.

I won't stand a chance, Kristi thought, but still, I've got to try.

Two

SARA came to South Bay in the middle of the morning. She was smaller and just a little heavier than she looked in photographs.

Kristi knew that skaters sometimes put on a few extra pounds when they weren't on a full schedule. Maybe Sara isn't practicing full-time, she thought. Maybe her leg is really still bothering her.

Kristi was in the middle of her patch, a portion of the ice surface she rented for an hour at a time. She'd been working on a set of compulsory figures, special moves that all the skaters would be required to perform during the competition next month. One of the figures had been giving her trouble all morning. But now her concentration drifted away as she watched Sara and her mother walk beside the rink, shaking hands and talking to people.

Kristi frowned. Must be nice, she thought, to have your mother lead the way when you go to a new rink. Sara's mom probably does everything for her. All Sara has to do is look pretty and win championships. Kristi bit her tongue. She knew she was thinking mean thoughts.

She looked around the rink. Young mothers with their small children in tow were arriving and putting on skates for the Mothers' Hour, which began at 9:30. Mothers' Hour was Mr. Billings' idea. He wanted to get more people in for public skating. But he hadn't counted on the kids who came along and were either too small to skate or just didn't want to. When Mothers' Hour first began, the children tore around the arena with nobody watching. Then Mrs. Billings took over as a baby-sitter. She tried to keep the kids in the lobby area, but that was hard for her to do. She also had to help out in the office at the same time.

"Hey," Becky called to Kristi from the next patch. "Look who's taking over." She nodded toward Mrs. Mars, who was surrounded by coaches and mothers and was now calling Sara to her side.

Sara turned this way and that, at her mother's direction, to show off her skating dress. Maybe her mother made it, Kristi thought. Some mothers did things like that.

Kristi turned away and pushed off into a strong forward edge again. When she had completed a spin, she stopped and leaned over to look at the tracings her skates had made. Good, she thought. That's better.

"Kristi!" She looked up when she heard her name called. Mr. Billings was waving at her, so she skated quickly to the edge of the rink.

"Mr. Billings, I'm in the middle of my patch," she began. "I'll be finished soon."

"This will only take a minute," he said. His thin

mustache twitched nervously. "Mrs. Mars wants you and Sara to meet."

Not like this, Kristi thought, feeling suddenly shy. I don't want to meet her in front of everybody. But Kristi skated down the rink so that she and Sara faced each other.

"Sara, this is Kristi Cameron. Kristi, Sara Mars," Mr. Billings said.

"Hi." Kristi tried to think of something else to say, something cool or clever. But the words stuck inside her.

"That bracket you just laid down looked really terrific," Sara said. She smiled at Kristi.

"Thanks. I've been having trouble with it all morning." Kristi looked closely at Sara's pink skating dress with its fur collar and cuffs. No wonder her mother was showing the dress off to the others. If that's what Sara wears for practice, I wonder what she wears for competition, Kristi thought. Kristi suddenly felt self-conscious about the old skating dress she was wearing.

"I'm glad the rink isn't crowded," Sara said,

looking out on the ice.

She sure is pretty, Kristi thought, trying not to stare. That haircut makes her seem older. And her skin is so clear. She's just perfect, except . . . except for her eyes. For some reason, Sara's eyes reminded Kristi of a scared rabbit.

Mrs. Mars finished talking to a coach and turned around. "This is my mom," Sara said.

"Is your mother here, Kristi?" Mrs. Mars asked. "I'd love to meet her. After all, if you girls are going to compete for the championship . . ."

"My mother doesn't come to the rink," Kristi said. "She works."

Sara tapped her fingers on the railing and looked at her mother impatiently.

"Then who is your manager?" Mrs. Mars asked. "Your coach?"

"My coach just had a baby," Kristi said. "It'll be a while before she comes back to work."

"But what about your lessons?" Mrs. Mars was insistent. "I mean, how can you get ready for a competition unless you have regular lessons?"

"Mom." Sara's voice had an edge to it. "It's none of our business."

"That's okay," Kristi said. "I'm looking for a new coach right now." But she wished Mrs. Mars would stop asking so many questions. "If you can think of someone who has some spare time, maybe you'll let me know."

"We'll ask around," Sara said. "There must be a coach here who has some free time."

"Thanks. See you later," Kristi said. She glided backward to the center of the rink as she called out, "Did you bring your lunch? Some of us eat together every noon and . . . ."

"Oh, Sara has to rest during her lunch break," Mrs. Mars said. "I'm afraid that's out of the question."

As Sara's mother turned away, Kristi saw a strange, unhappy look flash through Sara's eyes. It was a look of either anger or fear, Kristi wasn't sure. *Something* was definitely bothering Sara. What was it?

Sara's got everything, Kristi thought. Talent,

money, and looks. And she's a shoo-in to win the regional novice competition. What could be wrong?

Three

SEVERAL afternoons later, as Kristi was leaving the rink, she spotted Becky and Matt about a half block down the street.

"Wait up!" she called. They turned and watched her run toward them in the late afternoon sunshine. Her skate bag pounded on her hip as she ran.

"Hurry up, Kristi, or we'll miss the bus," Becky urged. When Kristi caught up with them, they continued down Western Avenue together.

"Did Mr. Billings give you the word this afternoon?" Kristi asked.

"About the rink having to raise its rates and charge more money for ice time?" Matt asked.

"Yeah. I guess Dad won't yell too much. He always says skating's not as expensive as some other sports—like skiing."

"My grandmother pays for my skating time," Becky said. "I guess this increase won't break her."

"We know one person who won't be affected." Matt cleared his throat.

"Sara Mars, you mean?" Becky asked. "Have you been noticing her clothes these last couple of days? Wow, and have you checked out those neat skates? They're the most expensive ones I've ever seen."

"And the way she skates," added Kristi. "Have you ever seen anything like it?"

"I have," Matt said. "You skate just like her, Kristi, only better."

Kristi smiled. Matt was trying to be nice. She wished it were true. Maybe, if she had everything done for her like Princess Sara . . . .

"Hey, Kristi, what about you?" Matt asked. "Do you think your mom can swing the extra

money for your ice time?"

"I'm not sure," she said. "Have either of you heard anything about skating scholarships?"

"Scholarships?" Becky repeated. "You mean, there are such things for skating?"

"Sure are," Matt said. "I've read about them in *Skate and Spin* magazine. Rich people and organizations sometimes help out poor athletes. You have to be super good, though, to get a scholarship."

"That's Kristi." Becky linked her arm through Kristi's. "She's super good."

They stopped at the corner, and Kristi watched the bus roll up for them.

Becky suddenly looked worried. "You won't have to quit, will you? I mean, that would be awful if you had to stop skating because you couldn't afford it. You're too talented. Gosh, I can't do anything right on the ice. If anyone should be able to keep this up, Kristi, it's you."

They hopped on board. Kristi turned her face away from Becky and Matt so they couldn't see the tears that flooded her eyes. What would she do if she couldn't skate? The competition was so close now. It would be horrible to miss it. She had worked hard to pass the tests and to prepare a freestyle program. She'd designed her freestyle routine herself. In fact, she'd done most of the work without a coach. It wasn't fair. It just wasn't fair. She *had* to compete for the novice title, especially now that she'd met Sara. She couldn't let that girl get away with the championship as if she owned it.

Kristi got off the bus first. "I'll see you tomorrow," she called without looking at Becky and Matt. I hope, she added to herself, as she watched the bus continue down the street.

Kristi cut across the neighbor's lawn and hurried up to her front porch. The mail was still in the box. That meant her mother must be working late again.

Kristi picked up the mail, unlocked the door, and then headed for the kitchen. The house always seemed so empty with her mother gone.

Kristi looked in the refrigerator and wondered if she should start making tacos out of the hamburger. No, I'd better wait for Mom, she thought.

Upstairs in her room, she changed her clothes. Then she got out all her copies of *Skate and Spin* magazine. If she could find any scholarship ads, she'd apply right away, maybe tonight. She couldn't cut her ice time now, just a few weeks before the competition.

Kristi selected the May issue, and turned immediately to the article about Sara. "Novice Skater Begins Comeback," the title stated. Although Kristi had read the story many times, she read it again, now and then looking at the photograph of Sara with her coach, Jack Barrett.

I must be crazy to think I have a chance to beat her, Kristi thought.

"Kristi, are you upstairs?" Her mother's voice floated up from the hall.

"I'll be right down," she called.

"No, I'll come up," her mother said. "I want to tell you something."

Kristi flipped through the rest of the magazine but found only one scholarship offer, and that was for pairs skaters. After dinner she would go through the rest of her magazines. There had to be something for her.

Her mother came into her bedroom. "Hi, Mom. How was work today?" Kristi asked.

Kristi's mother turned, her eyes bright and excited. "Kristi, remember the man at the office I've told you about? Well, we got to talking . . ."

Kristi suddenly had a cold, clammy feeling in the pit of her stomach. She wasn't ready for her mother to start dating. But she knew it was coming. She'd felt it for weeks. Mom had been acting so weird, sort of like she was a teenager again.

"He's picking me up at seven for dinner," her mother finished. "I hope you don't mind, Kristi."

"No." Kristi's voice wavered. "But I need to talk to you for a minute."

"Go ahead. Why don't you talk while I get ready?" Kristi's mother said. She hurried into the bathroom and began to run her bath. Kristi tried to talk above the splashing sounds, but she knew her mother didn't hear her. In Mom's state, Kristi thought, she probably wouldn't hear me if I were standing right next to her and speaking into a microphone.

Kristi sighed. She guessed she'd have to ask her mom about the money problem another time.

Four

IT was early in the morning, and Kristi was the
only one on the ice. She loved practicing at
this hour. No one was around to distract her or
make her feel self-conscious. The sound of her
blades cutting the ice seemed to be the only
sound in the world.

She finished her warm-up exercises and
swirled to a stop. Why not try a triple toe-loop?
Nobody would see her if she couldn't complete
the figure. Think it through first, she told herself
as she paced out on the ice in strong, smooth
strokes. You've been doing singles and doubles
for a long time now. But a triple—that's another
story. Not too many kids have triples in their pro-

grams. But Sara probably does, Kristi thought.

Kristi quickly moved onto the back outside edge of her right skate and rotated her body once, twice, three times in the air before coming down on the same back outside edge. She held the edge without a wobble and started to smile. *You did it,* she told herself. *You did it!* Her smile grew to a grin. She could almost feel her freckles stretching.

"Kristi, that was really terrific. I just love to watch you skate."

She glanced up and saw Sara skating toward her. Kristi frowned.

"That was great!" Sara went on, her dark eyes shining. "How long have you been doing triples?"

"A couple of weeks." Kristi stopped skating to take several deep breaths. "I've been trying to decide if I should put a triple toe-loop in my freestyle program."

"Oh, you just have to," Sara said. "You can't leave it out."

"How many triples do you do?" Kristi asked.

"Well . . . ." Sara hesitated. "I'm not doing them right now. My leg is still bothering me a little."

"Gosh, I'm sorry." They began to skate on the ice together. "What happened?" Kristi wondered if the magazine version of the accident was correct.

"I landed wrong on one of my stunts," Sara said. "I twisted my leg and did something to the cartilage in my knee. But the doctor says it's okay to practice."

Kristi knew that it was tough to skate with a knee injury. "You'll be ready for the competition, won't you?" she asked.

Kristi caught a glimpse of that strange, unhappy look in Sara's eyes. "Oh, yes," Sara said quietly. "I have no choice. At least that's what my mother says. I suppose she's right." Sara then whirled and began to skate backward facing Kristi. "Do you always come this early?"

"Ice time doesn't cost as much before seven in the morning," Kristi answered. "But I haven't seen you here this early until today."

"Mom had to take the car in for a repair and she dropped me off," Sara said. "She'll be back pretty soon. She never misses a day at the rink." Sara gave a tired sigh as she spoke.

Kristi looked closely at Sara. Doesn't she want her mother to come? Just once, Kristi thought, it would be great if her own mom came. Or if she would at least act interested, even if she couldn't come to the rink. The night before, when Kristi had tried to tell her about the scholarship idea, her mother had just cut off the conversation.

"You'll have to quit, I'm afraid," she had said. "We can't afford to have you skate anymore, even though I know how much figure skating means to you."

"But, Mom, scholarships . . ."

"Kristi, I'm running late. Can we talk some other time?"

"When? When do we ever talk anymore?" Kristi's voice raised to a high pitch.

Her mother had looked at her a moment, as if

it were the first time in a year or two. "I guess I have been neglecting you," she had finally said.

Kristi stared out on the ice and threw herself into a spin. I'm not quitting, she thought. I'll get the money somehow. I'm going to be a champion one day, just like Sara. Anybody knows that champions never quit.

"You know what I'm going to do?" Sara said as she stopped suddenly in a spray of ice before Kristi. "I'm going to ask Mom if I can come in early, too. I can use the extra practice. Besides, it's so much quieter at this time of the morning without all those little kids."

"That would be great," Kristi said. "I'd learn a lot just by watching you." The compliment slipped out, surprising Kristi. But she meant it.

Sara smiled. "I think Jack would like it better, too," she said.

"Who's Jack?"

"My coach," Sara said.

Now Kristi remembered. She'd seen his picture with Sara in *Skate and Spin*. "Why do you think he would like it better?"

"He said I need to concentrate more, but that's impossible with all those little kids running around. They really ruin the patch I have just before the Mothers' Hour. Mrs. Billings can't really control them and help run the office at the same time," Sara said. She spun in the middle of the ice.

"Their noise bothers me, too," Kristi said, skating around her. "I don't know why they can't be left at home with baby-sitters."

"Baby-sitters cost money," Sara replied. "The mothers probably can't afford to skate and have baby-sitters, too."

"You're probably right," Kristi said. She, of all people, could understand money problems. She circled the ice as Sara continued to warm up.

Suddenly, Kristi's face lit up.

"I have a great idea!" she yelled to Sara.

Sara stopped skating. "What did you say?"

"Have you seen Mr. or Mrs. Billings come in yet?" Kristi shouted.

"We just walked in the front door." Mr. Billings stood at the edge of the rink, his hands on his hips. Mrs. Billings leaned over the rail, next to him. "What are you shouting about, Kristi?"

"I've got the greatest idea!" Kristi said as she skated over to them. "Can I talk to you both for just a minute?"

"Yes, if you hurry. I've got an appointment in 15 minutes. Come into my office," said Mr. Billings.

"I'll be right there!" Kristi hurried off the ice and slipped on her skateguards.

"I'll be back in just a second, Sara," she called. "Wait until you hear my great plan."

Five

SEVERAL mornings later, Kristi laced on her skates and thought about the scene in the manager's office.

"What you need is a baby-sitter for all the kids during the Mothers' Hour," she'd said. "Then Mrs. Billings can give all her attention to the office."

Mr. Billings mustache had begun to twitch. "I know, but I can't afford to hire anyone."

"I'll baby-sit for you all summer, and I won't charge a cent." Kristi hoped that she sounded more confident than she felt. "If you let me have my early morning patches free."

Mrs. Billings had looked like she was going to hug Kristi. Instead, Mr. and Mrs. Billings had beamed at each other and said she could start work immediately. And she did.

Now, Kristi skated out on her free morning patch. She was happier than she'd been for days. Not only was she helping to pay her own skating expenses, she was learning a lot from Sara, too. Since Mrs. Mars had agreed to let Sara come earlier, the two girls shared a second early morning patch together. Kristi was beginning to enjoy Sara's company. Kristi enjoyed talking to someone who was as dedicated as she was.

But the first hour still belonged to Kristi alone, and she wanted to make the most of it. In her freestyle program, she could really let herself go. She flew around the ice, trying new combinations, jumping into spins, and leaping out of them in her own individual style. Without a coach, of course, it was hard to spot her own mistakes, but she'd have to do it. She wanted to win the regional competition. She wanted to be number one.

Finally she felt warmed up. She skated over to

put her tape on the sound system. It began with the "Overture" from *Romeo and Juliet*. Kristi liked to glide along in her spiral as the violins played. Next came the fast music. Kristi zipped along, putting in a lot of tricky footwork. That felt really good! And she was right on the beat. Now came a double Lutz and then a double axel. Oops, a little slip on the axel—she'd have to work on that stunt. Now into a layback spin as the music slowed down, and finally a strong scratch spin at the end. She stopped herself in a spray of ice and bowed to the imaginary judges and audience.

"Very good," a man's voice called from the edge of the rink. There was the sound of someone clapping. "Very good. You've got to land that axel better, though."

Kristi nearly jumped out of her skates at the sound of the man's voice. She shaded her eyes, hoping to catch a glimpse of him, but she couldn't see beyond the glare of the rink.

"Thanks," she called, skating over to the sound

system outlet to get her tape.

"I'm Jack Barrett," he said, coming toward her.

Now Kristi could see him. Of course—Sara's coach! He must be waiting for Sara to arrive.

"I'm Kristi Cameron," she said.

"Sara's friend," he said. His dark eyes were warm and sparkling. "She told me what an excellent skater you are, but I had to come and find out for myself."

Kristi couldn't find her voice. "You mean," she finally managed, "you came down here to see me?"

"I'll be coaching Sara when she gets here, but she gave you a good buildup and said you needed a coach . . ."

So that's it, Kristi thought. He wants me to hire him. "I'm sorry," she said. "I don't have any money for coaches. I can barely afford patch time." She began to skate toward the gate.

"That's too bad," he said. He took off a heavy sweater and threw it on a bench. "A girl of your talent trying to compete without proper coaching—that's a shame." He walked along beside the rink as she skated. "Will you let me help you at least until the novice competition?"

"But I can't pay you," Kristi said. Why couldn't he understand?

"We'll worry about that when you're rich and famous." He grinned at her. "Besides, since Sara is usually late, I think that ten minutes a morning wouldn't hurt." He hopped over the railing in his street shoes. "Come on," he said. "Let me see your freestyle."

Kristi stood there, unable to move. Things were happening so fast she was afraid she'd wake up and find it was all a dream.

"I've heard about a scholarship that will be available in a few months. If you work hard, you may be eligible to try for it," Jack said, waiting for her.

Then Kristi leaped into motion. "Okay," she said. "Here goes."

He began to explain. "Rotate your body more as you lift off the ice in that axel," he said.

"Remember to *spot*—keep your eyes on a fixed point—when you go into a spin. That way you won't travel."

Time passed so quickly that Kristi couldn't believe it when Sara skated up for her lesson.

"Practice your figures next, Kristi," Jack said. "I'll see you again tomorrow."

"Right. Thanks a lot, Jack," she said. And thank you, Sara, she thought. How can I ever thank you? Suddenly Kristi felt terrible about all the mean things she'd thought about Sara. Sara was really turning out to be something special.

Six

ON the morning of the competition, Kristi was awake and dressed before her alarm rang. She didn't even think about being scared until she was on her way to the bus. There would be plenty of time to worry later.

As she went inside the rink, she could hear the voices of the other kids who were waiting to be driven to the arena downtown, the site of the competition. She hurried to the manager's office.

"Okay, she's here," Matt announced. "Let's go."

"We have to get organized first," Mr. Billings said. "Have you all turned in your entry forms?"

There was a chorus of yesses from the kids who were pacing nervously around the room.

Suddenly the office door burst open and Sara rushed in. "Got room for one more passenger, Mr. Billings?" she asked.

"You're welcome to ride with us," Mr. Billings said. "But I thought—"

"Well, I decided to come with you," Sara interrupted.

"Is it okay with your mother?" Mr. Billings tried again.

"Sure, it's okay." Sara walked over and stood beside Kristi.

"How did you get down here, Sara?" Kristi whispered.

"I took the bus, just like you," Sara whispered back.

"I figured you were going to drive over to the arena with your mother." Kristi shifted her skate bag to her other arm.

"Where did you get that idea?" Sara asked. "Just because—"

The office door burst open again, and Kristi looked up to see Mrs. Mars. Everyone stopped

talking and stared, first at Mrs. Mars, then at Sara.

"Excuse me, Mr. Billings," Mrs. Mars began. "I wonder if I can speak to Sara."

Mr. Billings looked uncomfortable. "Yes, yes, of course. Sara, would you like to step out in the hall?"

But Sara didn't budge. "I'm going to ride in the van with the other kids," she blurted.

"Sara, you know you can't," Mrs. Mars said.

"I'll be okay, Mom." Kristi couldn't tell if Sara was going to get mad or start crying. One thing was certain—something was very wrong.

Mrs. Mars cleared her throat. "Sara, we're interrupting the meeting. Now come out here in the hall, and we'll talk."

Sara shook her head, but her shoulders seemed to droop. Kristi could see the expression on her face clearly. She *was* scared, really scared. But why would she be so frightened?

Then Sara ran out the door, and Mrs. Mars quickly followed her. Everyone was quiet, then

Mr. Billings began to cough nervously.

Becky came to stand by Kristi. "Sara's mom is really something," she muttered.

"Okay, everybody," Mr. Billings said, finding his voice. "Out to the van!"

Minutes later the group from South Bay was speeding north on the freeway toward downtown.

Kristi watched the cars whiz past while her thoughts whirled around in her head. She tried not to think about the scene between Sara and Mrs. Mars. Instead, Kristi focused on all that had happened to her the past couple of weeks, like Jack, for instance. His coaching had really improved her skating. An audience might not see the improvement, but the judges would pick it up. Her figures were sharper, and her freestyle program was something she felt very confident about. Jack had even made suggestions about her hairstyle and appearance. He had suggested orange for the color of her skating dress.

"Orange!" her mother had said that night. "You'll look like a popsicle. You're too thin." But she had offered to sew the dress, and Kristi appreciated that.

The two of them had selected a style with some fullness here and there to round out Kristi's slimness. Even her mother had been pleased with the results. "Not bad," she'd said. "Not bad."

Kristi thought about her mother. Mrs. Cameron had begun listening to Kristi once more, and helping her when she found time. Just the other day her mom had said, "For the first time in months, I feel so happy. Maybe now I can concentrate on being a better mother. I hope we'll understand each other better."

Kristi had just grinned back at her mother. Things had already seemed better.

Becky gave Kristi a sharp poke and brought her thoughts back to the present. "Are you nervous?"

"Butterflies are skating in my stomach," Kristi said.

"You don't need to worry," Becky said. "I've seen your freestyle routine and you're going to give Sara the best competition she's ever had. I'm sure glad you decided to leave the triple toe-loop in your program."

Kristi's thoughts leaped back to Sara. Something's bothering her, and I wish I could help, Kristi thought. Sara helped me by telling Jack to come and watch me skate. She must have known that Jack would coach me. Sara's a real friend. It's going to be hard competing against her for the championship, but I've got to try. We'll have to work extra hard to be friends everywhere else.

A half hour later Mr. Billings pulled into the parking lot of the downtown arena and stopped beside Jack Barrett's compact car. It was parked next to Mrs. Mars' station wagon.

Everyone grabbed skates and garment bags.

"I hope that you aren't going to wear that T-shirt when you skate," Kristi heard Becky say to Matt as they got out of the van. Matt had on an old, ratty T-shirt from a rock concert.

"Hey, it's my lucky shirt," Matt said jokingly, smiling Kristi's way. "I'm sure that the judges

won't mind if I wear it!"

As they approached the front door to the arena, it opened in front of them and Jack Barrett hurried out. He motioned for Kristi to come toward him.

Kristi knew from the look on Jack's face that something was wrong. "What happened?" she asked.

"Sara's disappeared," he said. "No one knows where she is, and Mrs. Mars wants to see you right away!"

Seven

"I thought Sara might have said something to you that would help me find her," Mrs. Mars said as Kristi faced her in a small, unused dressing room below the rink. "You and Sara have become such good friends over the last few weeks."

Kristi could see that Mrs. Mars had been crying.

"Mrs. Mars, I'm sure she hasn't had time to go very far." Kristi tried to sound reassuring. "She's probably wandering around, talking to people. You know how she likes to talk about skating. You'll find her."

"No," Mrs. Mars said, shaking her head. "I've

asked everyone who's been here since we came. We hurried right over from South Bay. We always arrive early before a competition."

"Why?"

"So that Sara can rest. She gets so nervous and worked up that she has to lie down. I left her in the dressing room and went out to talk to someone. When I came back, she was gone. No one has seen her since."

Kristi swallowed hard. She decided to ask a question that might make Mrs. Mars angry. "Was she mad because you wouldn't let her ride with us?"

Mrs. Mars looked up, frown lines gathering on her face. Then she smiled weakly. "I know you kids think I was mean to make Sara ride with me. But she gets carsick when she rides in the back of a van. She always has." Mrs. Mars dabbed at her eyes with a handkerchief. "I don't know why she wanted to try it again."

Try what? Kristi wondered. Riding in a van or . . . Kristi began to have the feeling she got sometimes when she was reading a book and tried to skip to the last chapter. She'd always miss something in the story and then have to go back and read what she'd missed. Now she felt like she'd missed something about Sara. What was it? She tried to skip back in her mind to see if she could figure out the answer. But it wouldn't come.

"Run along," Mrs. Mars said, forcing a smile. "You've got your compulsory figures to do pretty soon."

"But Sara has compulsories the same time I do," Kristi said. "She should be getting ready now, too. I'll just look around a few minutes before I start to dress."

Kristi entered the dressing room assigned to her. Becky and four other girls were putting on their skates, dresses, and a little makeup. Kristi threw her skate bag on a chair in front of the dressing table and then hung her garment bag on a wall hook.

"What's going on?" Becky asked, combing her

long, dark hair and making faces at herself in the mirror above the table. "You look like you just lost the competition."

"Nerves, I guess." Kristi decided not to say anything about Sara's disappearance yet. After all, there might be a logical explanation.

"I'll be right back." Kristi wanted to look for Sara quickly before they both missed their events.

She closed the door of the dressing room behind her and stood in the long, dim corridor, wondering which way to go. The downtown arena was much larger than South Bay, and she wasn't familiar with it. There were so many rooms, for instance, opening off this hall. They had to be dressing rooms. Most were full of kids getting ready to compete.

Kristi walked slowly down the hall, listening. From behind most of the closed doors, she could hear talking, a giggle or two, even nervous shrieks of laughter. No, Sara wouldn't be in any of these rooms, not if she wanted to hide.

Then Kristi stopped. Why would Sara want to hide? Why would she disappear? "Because she doesn't want to skate," Kristi said aloud. That had to be it. What other reason could there be?

But why would a skater as good as Sara not want to skate? Was Sara so mad at her mother that she would throw away her chances in the competition? No, that wasn't like Sara at all. She loved skating, everything about it.

Everything, Kristi slowly realized, everything but competing. That's it. Sara wasn't afraid of her mother. She was afraid of competing.

But she would be watching somewhere, even if she didn't participate. She loved the sport that much.

Now Kristi had an idea. She ran quickly up the stairs and found herself standing in the huge, dimly lit arena. Spectator seats rose all around the rink, way up nearly to the rafters. Skaters were everywhere, walking around and talking to one another. None of them would be sitting still except Sara, Kristi knew . . . if Sara was there.

Kristi looked up to the highest row of seats. She let her eyes follow the line of chairs all the way around the rink. It wasn't long before she found what she was looking for. She took the aisle steps two at a time all the way to the top.

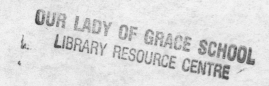

Eight

SARA was watching as Kristi worked her way across the row of seats at the top of the dark stadium. Kristi flopped down beside her.

"How did you know where to look?" Sara asked. "I didn't want anyone to find me until after the competition. Then I would have come down."

"You also would have been disqualified," Kristi said.

"That's exactly what I had in mind." There were tears in Sara's eyes.

Kristi's voice shook as she spoke. "But you're the champion. Champions don't quit."

"This one does," Sara shot back. "I'm afraid to

compete any more."

So I was right, Kristi thought. She's afraid, but maybe she has a good reason. "Is it because of your leg?" Kristi asked. "Are you afraid it won't support you?"

"No, my leg's fine," Sara replied. "I usually get nervous before each competition, only this time it's worse. I even wanted to ride in the van. Then maybe I'd get sick."

Now Kristi realized that Sara was having a severe case of stage fright.

"All athletes get nervous before competing," Kristi said. "Baseball players get themselves all worked up and so do runners and football players. They say it helps them perform better."

Sara watched the skaters warming up on the ice down below. Then slowly and quietly she said, "Everyone expects me to be the best again, just because I'm the champion. It's just too much pressure. I'm not that good."

"But you are," Kristi said. "Someday I hope I can skate as well as you can."

Sara slipped down farther in her seat and closed her eyes. She clasped her hands together.

If I don't say the right thing pretty soon, Kristi thought, I'll never convince her that she's got to skate.

"Please, Sara," she said. "Please skate in the competition."

Sara opened her eyes and looked at Kristi. "Why? It will be a lot easier for you if I don't. There's not another novice skater here who can come close to beating you. If I don't skate, you'll be the champion." She closed her eyes again.

She's right, Kristi thought. I'm the only challenger that Sara has for the title. And I'll be sure to win if she doesn't skate. It would be so easy just to walk away, to leave her sitting here. Then I would go on to win the competition. Sure, I could do it. But that would be cheating. I don't want to be champion that way.

Then Kristi realized what she had to tell Sara. "That's not fair," she said. "You're not being fair to me, Sara Mars. If you don't skate, then I'll

never know how good I am. I've got to beat a champion to become one."

Sara looked at her for a long time. Finally a smile began to play at the corners of her mouth.

"Competition starts in ten minutes," Kristi said. "Come on. I'll race you to the dressing room."

They dressed quickly and were on the ice just as the judges made the official announcement beginning the competition. Kristi and Sara took their assigned patches and began the series of figures that each skater was required to do. Kristi concentrated, never once looking up to see how anyone else was skating.

As the morning and afternoon went on, skaters came off the ice and were replaced by others who maneuvered through the figures. Kristi stayed by herself in a spectator seat when she was not competing, and Sara did, too. Once Becky tried to talk, but Kristi didn't answer. Becky got the message and left her alone after that. Kristi saw Matt looking anxious as he prepared to skate.

Then it was evening and time for the freestyle event, the most popular part of the competition. Family and friends crowded into the arena.

Kristi wondered if her mother had managed to come to the program. She probably had a date or something, Kristi thought. But that was all right. Her mother had a right to make new friends, too. Kristi knew she wouldn't like it if her mother bustled around her all the time, the way Mrs. Mars bustled around Sara.

During the compulsory figures, Sara had pulled slightly ahead of Kristi in the standings. In the freestyle portion of the competition the two girls were evenly matched. If either of us makes a serious mistake, Kristi thought, the other is sure to win the competition.

Sara skated first. Kristi watched as she skated beautifully. Sara didn't look nervous, but Kristi knew that she had to be shaking inside. That's courage, Kristi thought. Sara ought to get first for courage alone.

At last it was Kristi's turn. She breathed

deeply and tried to ignore the terrified feeling in the pit of her stomach as she skated out on the ice. She knew that her high jump combinations, fast spins, and long spiral were sure to get top marks from the judges if she didn't goof.

Suddenly the "Overture" to *Romeo and Juliet* exploded through the sound system. As she threw herself into her first set of tricky moves, her fear melted away. The crowd clapped and cheered for her. Listen to that applause, she told herself. They really like me!

Then it was time for Kristi's triple toe-loop. She tried to concentrate extra hard as she shifted her weight onto the back outside edge of her right skate, then rotated her body once, twice, three times in the air. She heard the crowd go wild.

But as Kristi came down on her right skate, she felt her ankle wobble. Suddenly she was falling, out of control, on the ice. Her fingertips scratched across the cold surface as she skidded to a stop. Without waiting to catch her breath, she picked herself up and began skating again, trying to keep up with the music. The crowd applauded her attempt, but tears still gathered in her eyes. All she wanted to do was cry—to run away to some dark place and scream at herself for including the difficult move in her program. She shouldn't have tried the triple! She hadn't perfected it yet.

Seconds later, Kristi's program concluded with a fast scratch spin. The audience gave her a standing ovation, but Kristi knew Sara had won.

"You were great!" Sara hugged Kristi as she stepped off the ice.

"Thanks." Kristi's breath came in short spurts. "Thanks a lot."

Jack ran up to them and brought flowers. "From your mother and her date," he said to Kristi. He pointed to them in the audience, and Kristi waved through a blur of tears.

Thanks, Mom, she thought. Thanks for everything.

The judges began their official announcements.

Becky received fifth place in the Intermediate division for girls, and Matt was third in the boys' competition. Then came the announcement Kristi was waiting for.

"In the novice division, the winner of the silver medal is Kristi Cameron of South Bay." Kristi skated out to the center of the rink to receive her medal and take her place on the second tier of the winner's platform.

"In first place, novice division, the winner of the gold medal is Sara Mars, also of South Bay." The announcer's voice bounced around the stadium through the loudspeaker.

As Sara skated out to join Kristi on the platform, the audience cheered and clapped again. Kristi looked around and waved with one hand, while holding her flowers cradled in her other arm.

"Isn't this terrific?" Sara whispered to her as they waved to the crowd. "Thanks Kristi, thanks for everything."

Kristi smiled. Maybe next year it would be her

turn to be first. She'd make it yet. She'd only begun to skate at the novice level, and she'd already come close to winning.

Right now, Kristi liked the way she felt inside. She and Sara had both tried as hard as they could to win. It had been a fair match, and they had ended up friends. There's much more to competing than being first, Kristi thought, so much more.

When the awards ceremony was over, Kristi and Sara joined hands and skated back to the dressing room. Both wore proud smiles.

About the Author

ELIZABETH VAN STEENWYK has written over 40 books for young people and more than 100 articles and short stories for adults' and children's magazines. She has also written and produced many radio and television programs for children.

Elizabeth was born in Galesburg, Illinois. Galesburg is the hometown of Carl Sandburg. Elizabeth read many of Sandburg's books at an early age.

"Students growing up there inherited a literary legacy," she has said. "That early influence gave me the hope that I, too, could become a writer one day. Fortunately, that's all I've ever done and I couldn't have wished for more."

When she is not writing, Elizabeth enjoys traveling with her husband to far off places. She also enjoys backpacking California's High Sierra, reading history and biography, tap dancing, and practicing magic.

Elizabeth and her husband have lived in San Marino, California for many years. They are the parents of four grown children.